A Different Dog

A Different Dog

Paul JENNINGS

with illustrations by
Geoff KELLY

ALLEN&UNWIN
SYDNEY•MELBOURNE•AUCKLAND•LONDON

First published by Allen & Unwin in 2017

Allen & Unwin
83 Alexander Street
Crows Nest NSW 2065
Australia
Phone: (61 2) 8425 0100
Email: info@allenandunwin.com
Web: www.allenandunwin.com

A Cataloguing-in-Publication entry is available
from the National Library of Australia
www.trove.nla.gov.au

ISBN 978 1 76029 646 9

Cover and text design by Sandra Nobes
Cover illustration by Geoff Kelly
Set in 12½ pt Minion by Sandra Nobes
Printed in Australia in August 2017 by Griffin Press

5 7 9 10 8 6 4

MIX
Paper from
responsible sources
FSC® C009448
www.fsc.org

The paper in this book is FSC® certified.
FSC® promotes environmentally responsible,
socially beneficial and economically viable
management of the world's forests.

To Ruth and Frank

One

The boy opened his eyes and saw that the
light globe was too high. It seemed to hover like
a low-flying eagle about to drop on a mouse. He
blinked his eyes to bring the morning into focus
and noticed that the ceiling was also higher than
it should have been. Then he remembered. And
realised.

It was not the ceiling that had moved. It was him. He was sleeping on a mattress on the floor.

His wooden bed had collapsed and his mother had chopped it up for firewood. He didn't really mind. It was cold inside and the flames had kept the place warm until morning.

But that was yesterday and there was no firewood left. He knew from the frost on the window that it would be another damp, chilly day.

He stood up quietly and pulled on his underpants and T-shirt. He shivered and quickly added a ratty pair of jeans and a holey jumper. Then he wriggled into his mother's pink parka. The one with the furry border around the hood. White stuffing poked out through a couple of holes in the sleeves.

'Everyone will laugh,' he said.

He pulled up the zip.

'But I don't give a rat's.'

He pulled out the black gar-bag that he had shoved under the mattress and pushed his head through the hole in the bottom. He pulled the rest of it down over his body and thrust his arms through the slits in the side.

He examined himself in the cracked mirror on the wall. They had found it on the side of the road. It had a sailing ship etched into the glass.

'Now I'll be okay if it snows,' he said. 'But I'll look like a fool.' He shook his head and gave a rueful smile.

'The Gar-bag Kid rides again,' he said. 'But at least it will keep me dry.'

The door of his mother's room was ajar and he could hear her gentle breathing.

'Today I will win some money,' he said to himself. 'And then Mum can buy two beds. And electric blankets. And we will fix the broken window. And she won't have to work in the orchard in the winter.'

More than anything he wanted her to get a job which didn't leave her with red raw hands and cold feet. A job inside. In the warm. That paid well.

'But what if you don't win?' he said. 'What then?'

He could see the fog of his own breath in the damp air.

'I *will* win,' he said. 'I have to. Because...'

He didn't finish the sentence. He knew that good jobs were hard to find in country towns. Especially for a single woman with a boy to look after.

He put on his worn boots and picked up the backpack that he had prepared the night before. Then he walked over to the outside door, quietly twisted the handle and stepped into the frosty morning. In the far distance the higher mountains were covered in snow. He could just make out the twisting road to the top of the nearest peak.

'Here I come,' he said. 'Ready or not.'

He walked across the bare paddock and

paused at the wire gate. He read the words scratched into the bark of the only tree on the property.

In Memory of Deefer

A distant sound like the breaking of a dry stick cracked across the valley.

The boy winced. It was that damned man again. Firing at the corellas. Scaring them off his newly sown field. Sending the flock into the air like a frightened white cloud.

Every morning in spring the man fired his gun into the air. The boy's mother called the gunshot 'The Morning Rooster' because it often woke her up.

Blinking back a tear the boy began his journey. He made his way along the deserted and lonely track to the main road, which led to the foot of the mountain. He passed the secondary school and then began his ascent. There was no one else to be seen.

He planned his strategy. The competitors would start at the lookout at the top of the mountain and jog to the bottom and then back up again. The final leg down would end at the school where there would be food and entertainment.

'I have to save my energy,' he said. 'It's going to take all day. Start off slow and just keep going.'

He sighed and looked up the steeply winding road...

'Who are you kidding?' he said. 'You'll be tired before you even start.'

For the first hour he had the road to himself. The left side fell away dangerously into the forest below. Bent trees struggled to gain a hold on the rocky banks.

He moved to the side at the sound of an approaching car. It was coming up from behind, headlights still on. He stepped nervously closer to the edge as the car slowed and then stopped.

The boy groaned as he recognised the late model SUV.

A window dropped and a grinning face appeared. It was Skinny Luke. The kid from Year 8C who was always trying to get him to talk.

'You have to ask,' said Skinny Luke.

The boy said nothing.

'Otherwise it's no ride,' said Skinny Luke.

The boy shook his head.

'It's talk or walk,' said Skinny Luke. He smirked, pleased with himself. He said it again. To make sure that they all got the joke.

'Talk or walk.'

'Love the parka,' said a voice from the back seat. 'Where did you get it?'

The boy saw that it was Skinny Luke's sister. She was wearing the latest snow gear.

The boy pressed his lips together and said nothing.

Skinny Luke's father leaned across to the open window.

'Hop in,' he said. 'We'll give you a lift.' The rear door swung open.

The boy shook his head.

'He can't get the words out,' said Skinny Luke.

'He only talks to one person,' said Skinny Luke's sister.

'Himself,' said Skinny Luke.

'Are you sure you don't want a ride, son?' said Skinny Luke's father. 'It's a long way to the top and you might miss the start.'

The boy shook his head again.

'He's stubborn,' said Skinny Luke. 'He can talk but he won't even try.'

'Leave him alone,' said Skinny Luke's father. He opened the glove box and fiddled around. He produced a pencil and a small notebook and held it out to the boy.

'Write it down,' he said. 'What you want to say.'

The boy shook his head again.

Skinny Luke's father put his notebook back in

the glove box. He gave the boy a smile and then said, 'Good luck in the race. I hope you win.'

The boy heard a snort from the back seat.

'Thanks heaps, Dad,' said Skinny Luke's sister.

The man turned around and spoke to his daughter. 'I'm putting up the prize money,' he said. 'And you don't need...'

His voice trailed off. He didn't want to go on. But the girl wasn't finished yet.

'I need the money,' she said. 'Just because he's poor doesn't mean that I...'

He frowned and barked out one word.

'Desist.'

There was silence in the car.

Their father leaned across and spoke to the boy.

'We're helping organise the race,' he said. 'The money is going to set up an op shop in town. To support the SES.'

The boy already knew this. It cost one hundred dollars to enter. Anyone could win but kids didn't have to pay. Most of the money went to the State Emergency Service.

The boy nodded and the man started the car

'Love the gar-bag,' said Skinny Luke.

The back door slammed and the car began to move off.

The boy heard muffled laughter and Skinny Luke's voice shouting.

'Talk or walk, talk or walk.'

He began to jog on but was forced to move to the side again as another car came up from behind. A red van with writing on the side. The driver showed no sign of stopping or even noticing the boy on the side of the road. Next to the driver was a dog, which, like its owner, was wearing earmuffs.

Instinctively the boy touched his own ears. He gave them a rub to ease the biting cold that was creeping through the thin hood of his mother's parka.

The dog sat in the passenger seat taking in

the scenery. It reminded the boy of the way his mother used to sit in the car, looking around. In the days when they had a car. Before she lost her job when the post office closed.

The boy smiled at the dog. It had sad eyes but it seemed to smile back.

And then the car was gone.

The boy jogged on for half an hour or so. Then he dropped his pace back to a walk, trying to ignore the stitch in his side and the pain that had developed in his left leg. The clouds were building slowly above him and he knew that he should turn around and head back home.

'It's a waste of time,' he said to himself. Then he spoke as if someone was listening.

'I'll never win. I'll never even get there. I should have gone in the car. But Skinny Luke is a pain.'

He bent over and panted like an athlete at the end of their run.

He straightened up.

'But I have to give it a go. For you, Mum. I'm going to win the thousand dollars. And get you all the firewood you need. And good shoes. And the best parka in the world. And you won't have to work in the orchard in the winter. And get sore hands. And walk all the way there.'

He wished he could tell her all this. All he wanted for her.

The road sloped steeply in front of him.

'Downhill is harder,' he said. 'It will be worse coming back. But not as tiring.'

Without warning, the clouds released their load. Hailstones bounced on the bitumen as if thrown by some hostile giant in the sky. He imagined the sound on the tin roof of the shed.

'It will wake Mum up,' he said. 'If the Morning Rooster hasn't done it already.'

He stood under a large gum tree and watched every exposed space turn white. The hail lasted for about five minutes and then stopped, leaving a river of icy beads twisting down the mountain.

'I'd better watch my step,' he said.

He picked up a handful of the stuff from the road and rolled it between his gloved fingers.

'Or I will go a sixer.'

He started to pick his way up the mountain. Treading carefully. Judging every step. Not wanting to feel his legs slide from under him.

Then he heard a sound from above. The unmistakable crunch of wheels. Moving fast.

He jumped to the side of the road. It was the red van coming back down the mountain.

'Don't hit the brakes, mate,' he said to himself.

The van rushed towards him, gaining speed with every second.

'Or you are a goner.'

The van flashed past with the rear wheels locked. It fishtailed a couple of times through the white hailstones and disappeared around the bend.

Two

The boy hurried down after the van, picking his way carefully. He rounded the bend and surveyed the stretch of road in front of him.

The road was empty. He knew that the van couldn't have made it to the next corner.

He went as quickly as he dared, careful. But not careful enough. His feet suddenly slipped out from under him and he crashed onto his backside.

'Rats,' he said. 'That hurt.'

He jumped up and continued on, following the crushed tracks of the van's wheels. From time to time he peered down the cliff face searching for signs of the missing vehicle. Halfway to the next bend he found them.

Unmistakable skid marks ended at the edge of the road. Freshly broken saplings and crushed ferns marked the van's passage down the slope. It had miraculously avoided the bigger gums as it crashed down the valley. Far below he thought he could see a smudge of red.

Without stopping to think he began slipping, sliding and skidding down the steep mountainside. The cold wetness from the soil and shrubs sank into his jeans. At times he had to climb down sheer embankments and cling to branches and roots to stop himself from tumbling.

He passed a crushed side mirror and a steaming exhaust pipe which had been ripped off in the van's descent.

He was vaguely aware of how difficult it was going to be to get back up to the road.

Now he could see the van. It was crumpled into a tree with both front doors hanging open. Steam was rising slowly from the radiator.

He wanted to rush to the scene but a feeling of dread slowed him almost to a standstill. What was he going to find? What could he do? What did he know? He was only a boy. Mangled fears stole his courage.

He couldn't take a step closer. He tried to move his feet but they were held in place as firmly as the roots of the silent trees. He did not want to see.

If only there was someone else to take over. If he had a phone he could call the SES for help. Not that a phone would work in the mountains. And even if it did he wouldn't be able to get a word out. Phones were the worst thing of all.

He gritted his teeth and forced his trembling legs towards the open driver's door.

Unwanted images flitted through his mind as he thought about what he might have to do. He mumbled half-forgotten CPR lessons.

'Push the chest. Blow into the mouth.'

The man was slumped forward. A small trickle of blood was already drying on his upper lip. His neck was bent sideways like a broken branch on a tree. The eyes were open and sightless.

The man's white knuckles were still clenched on the steering wheel. The boy gasped in horror. Tentatively he reached out and raised the nearest hand. He felt the limp wrist.

'Nothing,' he said. 'There's no pulse. Or don't I know how to find it?'

He released the hand and it flopped down onto the man's lap. He knew what he was looking at.

Death.

He fell back and sprawled on the damp earth, screwing up his eyes, mumbling to himself, trying to block out the sight.

The sound of cars far above turned from a trickle to a steady stream as the kids from school and their parents headed up the mountain for the start of the race.

He opened his mouth and began the hopeless fight for words. He tried to call out 'Help'. But nothing came. His mouth was jammed open like a wooden clown in a sideshow waiting for a ball to be dropped down its throat. He tried to scream, but still nothing.

Remnants of the sight that he had just seen floated through his head like pieces of a torn photograph. He pushed them aside but they were immediately replaced by new images of the dead man's stare. Intrusive, wandering thoughts. About eyes.

Dead eyes.

Dull eyes.

Dolls' eyes.

Dogs' eyes.

Dogs' eyes?

'The dog,' he shouted. 'Where is the dog?'

The boy jumped to his feet and began searching the drooping undergrowth. He parted bushes and fought low scrub. Tree ferns showered him as he bumped and pushed his way through the unfriendly forest.

Finally he found the dog.

'There you are,' he shouted. 'But are you...?'

He couldn't say the word. The dog lay on its side, legs sticking out stiffly. The boy stood, staring.

'I can see your breath steaming, dog,' he said. 'You're alive.'

The dog's eyes were closed.

He knelt down and stroked its head.

'Wake up, fellah. Wake up. Please.'

The dog continued to breathe gently, its chest rising and falling. It was shaking from the cold.

The boy took off his tattered gar-bag and then his mother's parka. He put the pink parka over the dog and threaded its front legs through the sleeves. Then he folded the sleeves back and used the wrist cords to hold them in place. He pulled the fur-lined hood over the dog's ears and tied it in place with the chin-strap.

'I'm sorry,' he said. 'But I can't find your earmuffs.'

He put the gar-bag back on and sat by the side of the dog, stroking the fur of its neck and giving it a gentle massage.

Time passed. The boy started to shiver beneath his gar-bag. He walked over to the van and reached out to take the man's earmuffs. But his hands shook.

'It's no good,' he said to the unconscious dog. 'I just can't.'

The boy looked up at the cliff he had scrambled down and shook his head.

'No one will know that we're here, fellah,' he said. 'We're out of sight.'

Watery sun struggled through the branches. The hail on the ground had melted and only the deepest patches were left. His shoulders shook as he began to cry. He sobbed for the dog, for the dead man and for his own inability to make things right.

After a long time he heard the sound of distant voices. He wiped his cheeks and looked up towards the unseen road. The race had begun. The runners were making their way down the mountain. Hundreds of them. He imagined them picking their way around the remaining patches of hail.

He opened his mouth again to shout. But nothing came. It never came.

'Why can't I do it, fellah?' he said. 'Why can't I get the words out?'

He stared at the van.

A thought began to burrow out from his brain.

'Yes, yes, yes. That's it.'

He ran over to the driver's dangling door and, trying not to look at the dead man, pressed the button in the centre of the steering wheel.

Nothing.

He pressed again, frantically. Time after time after time.

Nothing.

Nothing.

Nothing.

Like himself, the car could not speak. The horn was silent.

He looked around desperately.

'Yes, that will do.'

He picked up a moss-covered rock and began to bang it on the bent bonnet.

Clang, clang, clang.

Each strike rang through the trees and then faded. Absorbed by the wet forest like water soaking into a sponge.

He smashed the rock onto the metal until his fingers burned with cold.

'It's no good,' he said. 'They will never hear.'

He sat down again next to the dog where it still lay on its side, breathing gently, eyes closed.

'Don't die, dog,' he said. 'Please don't die.'

He stroked its head with shaking hands.

'Can you hear me, dog?' he whispered. 'I know you are alive.'

The dog suddenly opened its eyes. Confused. Looking at him. Unblinking.

'Good dog,' he cried out. 'Good dog.'

He began to feel the animal's soft fur, searching for injuries.

'Are you okay?' he said. 'Are you hurt?'

He examined each leg carefully. They were hard and strong. The dog began to stretch under his touch. He touched the soft skin around its neck. And the bony tail. The dog began to wag it. Then it licked his hand.

The boy discovered a lump behind the dog's ear. 'I think you're okay, fellah,' he said. 'You have been knocked out. But now you're back.'

The dog stood up and shook itself as if it had just emerged from a swim. It didn't seem to mind the pink parka.

Then it looked at the boy with sad, hopeful eyes.

'I have bad news for you,' the boy said. 'Are you ready, my friend?'

The dog continued to stare.

'You can't say anything, can you, dog?' he said. 'Like me.'

The dog's eyes turned to the car.

'I'm sorry,' the boy said. 'He is gone.'

Three

The dog walked slowly towards the van. It whimpered, and pawed at the leg of the dead man.

'It's no good, fellah,' said the boy. 'He's not going to move. He's...

He couldn't bring himself to say the word *dead*.

Instead he said, 'Passed on.'

The dog whimpered again and then sat on the damp ground. And stared expectantly as if waiting for advice.

The boy looked up at the steep cliff face and pointed.

'That's where we have to go,' he said. 'But it's very steep. We have go up there. Somehow or other. That's the way home.'

The dog gave one more whimper and began to walk downhill, as if rejecting the suggested route.

'Not down there. Home.'

The dog stopped and looked at the boy. Then it continued its journey, pausing every now and then to sniff the ground.

'Come back. Not that way. It's too far. And you might get lost.'

The dog paid no attention and vanished behind a clump of ferns.

The boy grabbed the backpack and then gave a little shiver.

He followed without thinking. He cared about the man but he had to save the dog. That was his only purpose as he plunged deeper and deeper into the dense forest.

The boy stumbled many times as he hurried after the dog. He worried that it would outpace him and disappear.

He mumbled to himself. 'Hang on a bit, dog. Wait up. Don't forget me. What's your hurry?'

The dog sniffed and snorted and panted and determinedly continued its journey.

Soon the boy lost all sense of where he was. It was dark and gloomy beneath the high trunks and green treetops. The only direction he could be sure of was down.

And suddenly he was on his own.

'Come back, dog,' he yelled. 'Don't leave me. I'll freeze. And so will you.'

There was no reply from the silent forest.

'I'm lost,' he said to himself. 'I could end up … here alone. Like the man.'

He looked around and up. One tree loomed above all the others.

'I won't move out of sight of that gum tree,' he said.

He began to walk in a circle, always keeping the lofty tree in sight.

'Where are you hiding, dog?' he said.

Minutes passed. Then an hour or more. He walked slowly, circling, pushing through the undergrowth.

'I'm looking for you, dog,' he called. 'Can you hear me? Or are you back at the road? Have you forgotten me? Left me? It's getting colder.'

The words had no sooner left his lips than he saw the dog. Standing still in a small clearing. Locked into position, its legs braced as firmly as those of a statue.

'Are you alive, fellah?' the boy said.

He ran over and hugged the dog but it did not respond.

'I can see your breath still steaming in the air,' he said as he had once before. 'And I can feel your heart beating.'

The dog gave no response. It stood there, rigid.

'It's okay, dog,' he said. 'It's just me.'

The dog's eyes stared. Unblinking.

The boy stood up and patted his hands against his thighs.

'Here, fellah,' he said.

But the dog didn't move.

'Okay, my friend,' said the boy. 'Be like that. See if I care. I'm going to sit down and wait. You won't be able to stand there forever.'

He looked for a dry patch and sat down with his back against a tree. Then he searched in his backpack and found the chicken and cheese sandwich he had packed the night before. He held it out to the dog.

'Here, fellah,' he said. 'Are you hungry?'

The dog remained in place, stiff and still.

The boy took a bite from the sandwich and chomped loudly.

'Delicious,' he said. 'This is a very nice chicken and cheese sandwich, dog. It's old cheese and dry chicken and stale bread. Because we're poor and Mum hasn't got much money for hamburgers and things. But I like this sandwich and so will you.'

He held it out and tried again.

'Any dog would like this sandwich. Come on, fellah, have a bite.'

Still the dog did not move.

'You are a stubborn dog,' said the boy. 'Here, have this.'

He tore off a piece of the sandwich and threw it to the dog. It fell short by about a metre.

The dog did not move. Not even an eyeball.

'Go on,' said the boy. 'It's yours.'

He slumped back against the tree.

'Maybe you're hurt,' he said.

He thought about it a bit more.

'Are you paralysed? Or are you in a coma? I'll wait.'

He closed his eyes, and soon was sleeping fitfully.

When the boy awoke he saw at once that the pale sun was no longer overhead, but had moved behind the treetops.

The dog was still standing in its rigid position. It was shivering violently.

'Maybe it's all in your mind,' said the boy.

He thought of something he had heard his mother say.

'Maybe you're having a mid-life crisis.'

He tried again.

'What's your name?'

The dog didn't even move its eyes.

'You made me chase you,' said the boy. 'So I will call you Chase. Chase the dog.'

The dog continued to shiver.

'If we stay here, Chase, we'll...' He didn't want to use the terrible word.

'We have to go,' he said.

He stomped his icy feet and jogged on the spot, rubbing his hands while he did so. Then he picked up the scrap of sandwich that he had thrown to the dog and chewed it slowly. He carefully wrapped the rest of the sandwich and put it back in his pack.

'Come on, Chase,' he said. 'The time has come.'

He squatted down, put his arms beneath the dog and stood up.

'You're heavy, Chase,' he said. 'But you're not a burden.'

He began to walk, taking each step carefully down the slippery embankment.

'I can't carry you uphill,' he said. 'So we have to go down.'

The forest was unfamiliar. And the going was difficult, with closely packed undergrowth often blocking his way. He continued his descent with the dog held to his chest.

'You're getting heavier, Chase,' he said. 'I need a rest.'

He carefully put the stiff dog onto the ground where it stood on its legs without moving. The boy listened for a friendly sound. But there was nothing.

Finally he said, 'I can only talk to myself. And animals. But here you are. You can't talk at all. If you weren't paralysed you could bark.'

They sat in silence for a long time.

Finally the boy said, 'Listen, I can hear something.'

The dog did not move.

'The river,' he yelled. 'Down there.'

He grabbed the dog and began to stumble down the steep slope.

'Be careful,' he said to himself. 'You can't fall. Not with Chase in your arms.'

He broke through a tangled net of vines and gasped. He was on the very edge of a high cliff. Far below, the mountain stream rushed on its way, swirling and splashing over rocks and fallen trees.

'Look, Chase,' he said.

Chase did not look.

The boy drew a deep breath and stared at the line of poles and beams, which crossed the river like the spine of a dead dinosaur.

'It's the old railway bridge,' he said. 'We learned about it in History.'

He continued, on and down, not wanting to reach the bridge because stepping onto it would almost certainly end in a fall. He listened for a friendly call or the chopping sound of a helicopter. He looked for a flash of orange from an SES jacket.

'They don't even know I'm gone,' he said to the silent dog.

He pushed forward and finally stumbled across the overgrown track. He looked uphill.

'It goes up to the old goldmine, Chase,' he said. 'And on the other side it goes back to the road. But first we have to cross the bridge.'

When he reached the remains of the bridge he saw that it was worse than he thought. The raging river rushed on its way far below the beams.

His knees wobbled at the thought of attempting to cross. The words of Skinny Luke crept into his mind – how he had told him to talk or walk.

'I can't do either,' he said to the stiff and silent dog. 'I can't talk properly when there are people listening.' He winced as the thought hit him like a slap on the face.

He stared into the forest and opened his mouth to yell. To cry out for help. But the words would not come. He began to tremble. His eyes bulged. His mouth was jammed open. It felt as if an invisible stick was holding his jaws apart. Not a sound came from his mouth.

He gave up the effort and looked down at the dog.

'I can't even call out the word *help* to someone who's probably not even there, Chase,' he said. 'But I *can* try to get over that bridge. And I will. We have to get to the road before dark.'

With the dog still shivering and frozen in his arms, the boy took a nervous step onto the first narrow beam.

Four

The drop to the river yawned beneath him. The single row of beams was terrifyingly high.

'Don't look down,' he said to himself. He had heard of that advice being given to people stuck in high places. But it was almost impossible to follow it.

Placing one shaking foot carefully in front of the other he began to move forward. One, two, three … eleven, twelve, thirteen steps. The beam was damp and slippery.

He started to wobble. He felt the need to spread his arms like a tightrope walker, but how could he? The dog would fall.

'Chase,' he whispered. 'I can't let you go. But I can't go on with you like this. I'm losing my balance.'

He looked down at the rushing river.

'And we will both ... die.'

The terrible word turned his legs to jelly.

He bent his knees slightly and began to lower himself onto the narrow beam until he was in a squatting position. With trembling hands he held the dog out in front of him and turned it around so that it was facing the other side of the bridge. The dog was unbearably heavy in this position and the boy could not support the weight any longer.

'No,' he screamed as the dog slipped from his hands. It landed, still standing stiffly with each leg just on an edge of the narrow beam.

The boy knew that one puff of wind, one

vibration of the beam or one thoughtless movement would send the dog tumbling into space.

But he could not stay squatting for one second more. He fell down onto his knees and then lowered his backside onto the beam. Now he was sitting with his knees up under his chin. He dropped his legs so that he was straddling the beam.

The dog stood still, helplessly awaiting its fate. Frozen like a statue of ice. It stared along the line of beams to the other side with unseeing eyes.

The boy could not go forward without knocking the dog from its perch. And he couldn't turn around in his sitting position. All he could do was wriggle backwards.

He couldn't bear to look at the dog and watch it fall so he screwed up his eyes to shut out the world.

'I'm sorry, Chase,' he said. 'I can't help you. If I touch you it might make you fall.'

He dropped forward and let his arms droop

down on either side of the beam. Now all four limbs were hanging down, holding him in place. He rested his face on the splintery wood with his eyes closed, waiting, unable to watch the dog's inevitable fate.

'I can't talk and I can't walk,' he gasped. 'I can't talk and I can't walk.'

Seconds passed. Then minutes. His last word seemed to hang mockingly in the air.

The boy tried to distract his thoughts. He needed something to stop him from opening his eyes to the terrible sight of the raging river below.

'I'll tell you a story, Chase,' he said. 'A true story. If you listen carefully you might not fall.'

* * *

When I was little I had a dog. Not as big as you. But he was thin and fast. He could chase rabbits and even catch hares. Hares are hard to catch. They can change direction at full speed and the dog runs past them before it can stop and turn back.

I called him Deefer. Mum gave him to me on my sixth birthday. He was my dog.

At night Deefer was put on a chain in his kennel to stop him running away. He was not allowed off until Mum got up.

One morning while Mum was still asleep I went out to pat him. He was pulling at his chain. He wanted to get off. I felt sorry for him. So I let him go.

Right then a hare ran across the paddock. 'Come back,' I yelled. 'Come back.'

But Deefer did not come back. He went like a rocket after that hare. He was across the paddock and off down the road and gone.

I ran after him. I was only a little kid so I was slow. But I kept running. I ran and ran and ran. Soon I didn't know where I was. I was lost. I sat down and cried. I cried.

'Where are you, Deefer?' I said. I sat there on the side of the dirt road for a long time. I was tired. And thirsty.

Then I heard a voice. It was a man shouting. I walked through the trees and saw a little farmhouse. A man with a beard stood inside the fence of a chook run. He was yelling at Deefer.

I ran across the paddock. The man was picking up little ducklings. Seven little ducklings. They were all dead. And Deefer was crouching in the dust with his jaw on the ground. The man was yelling at him and Deefer was scared.

'Damn dog,' the man shouted. 'Damn dog, damn dog.'

He looked up and saw me.

'What happened to the little ducks?' I said.

'This damned dog killed them,' he said. 'They're pets. They belong to my kids. And they'll be coming home from school soon.'

He held out one of the ducklings. Its neck was flopping down and its eyes just stared.

'What will I tell my kids?' he said. 'The ducklings all have names. He started waving them at me. 'This one is Gingerbread. And this is Sam. And this is Little Mack.'

Deefer was still crouching down in the corner. He gave a squeal.

The man shouted, 'Someone is going to pay for this. I'll sue. I'll make them pay. The person who let this dog run around the countryside will pay.'

Then he stared at me.

'Is that your dog?' he asked.

'No,' I said.

'It's not yours?'

'No,' I said.

'Where do you live?'

I was frightened. I couldn't get the words out. I opened my mouth but nothing came.

The man looked at me. He didn't say anything more. I didn't say anything more.

He stepped out of the chook cage with the dead ducklings in his hands and used his bum to slam the gate shut.

Deefer was locked inside.

'Go home,' said the man. 'Go home and don't come back.'

I turned and ran. I ran across the paddock. I ran and ran and ran until I reached the road. I was lost. I walked along crying. Then I heard a loud noise. Like the crack of a breaking stick.

It was the Morning Rooster.

I stopped running. I stopped crying. I stopped thinking. There was nothing in my head. Nothing at all. I just walked and walked.

In the end I saw Mum coming the other way. She was crying. She gave me a big hug and said I was naughty for running off.

She said, 'Where's Deefer? Did you let him off the chain?'

I didn't speak. I didn't tell her.

She said, 'Never mind. He'll come home. He'll get hungry and come home.'

I didn't say anything. My feet were sore. Mum picked me up and carried me.

'You're heavy,' she said. 'But you're not a burden.'

Deefer did not come home. Ever. The Morning Rooster had taken him away.

Mum tried to get me to tell her what had happened. But there was nothing inside my head.

She took me to the doctor.

I tried to talk to him but I couldn't get the words out properly. I got stuck on 'dog'. I got stuck on 'duck'. And I got stuck on 'Deefer'. I couldn't talk properly.

I can sing. But you can't sing instead of talking. Or everyone will think you are nuts.

But I can talk to you, Chase. And other animals. But I get stuck with … people.

* * *

The boy still lay on the beam with his arms and legs dangling on either side. A gentle breeze brushed his face. He sat up with his eyes still closed and reached out a hand.

But he felt nothing. The air was empty.

He opened his eyes.

The dog had gone.

The boy looked down at the river far below but could not see Chase. He scanned the white water for any sign of a bobbing body. But he knew that it was hopeless. If the dog had fallen into the water it could not have survived.

Now nothing seemed to matter. The boy dropped forward again. He rested his face sideways, clenched his teeth and waited for the end.

His mind began to wander. An image of his mother floated into his mind. She would have been awake for ages now and would think he was running in the race.

The thought of a mattress on the floor and the remains of a bed burning in the fireplace seemed wondrous. He would give anything to be there, sitting in front of a fire. Especially if there was a loyal dog warming itself with him.

Something made him sit up.

He saw the dog.

It was walking along the edge of the cliff on the far side of the bridge. It was moving briskly up and down a small ledge. Each time it reached the end of the ledge it would turn and head back again in the other direction. It never paused for even a second.

The dog continued to pace in this way, moving confidently. It reminded the boy of someone striding back and forth trying to exercise in a small room.

He wanted to call out to the dog. But something told him not to. Instead he carefully raised himself onto his hands and knees. And began to crawl forward.

'I'm coming, Chase,' he whispered.

Crawling was still dangerous but not as bad as walking on the beam and carrying a dog at the same time. The boy tried to distract himself by watching Chase pace up and down on the small stretch of cliff.

Finally he reached the last beam, which he crossed at a snail's pace. He scrambled onto firm earth and fell on his face, kissing the damp soil.

'Made it,' he said.

Despite the fact that he was safe, the boy's heart sank as he looked around. The shelf was about as wide as a car and not much longer. A crescent-shaped cliff stood solidly in front of him like the wall of a prison. Behind him the river rushed and splashed at the foot of a sheer drop. There was no way down.

The dog continued to walk back and forth, unable to escape.

'Here, Chase,' he said.

The dog took no notice but kept walking briskly along the ledge, turning quickly each time it reached either end.

Half-buried railway sleepers marked out the remains of the old railway line. They crossed the narrow ledge and ended in a pile of rubble. At the top of the rubble he could see a black hole.

'A tunnel,' the boy said.

He scrambled up and peered in. All was dark but he could make out a small circle of light at the other end.

The dog continued to walk briskly without stopping. It was panting heavily, with its tongue hanging out. Saliva dripped from its mouth. The boy could tell that it was weary. He scrambled down.

'Stop, Chase,' he said. 'Come here.'

The dog continued to pace the cliff, its eyes staring ahead in tired desperation.

The boy was desperate too. 'It's stop or die,' he said.

He placed himself in front of the dog, held his arms apart and faced the other direction. He opened his legs and waited until the dog passed under him.

He grabbed the dog around its rib cage and straightened up.

'Gotcha,' he said.

The dog continued to walk with its legs swimming in the air, going nowhere.

'Stop,' yelled the boy. 'Stop, stop, stop.'

But the dog did not stop and the boy knew that he could not hold it for long.

The boy scrambled up the pile of rocks. He tried to shove Chase into the tunnel.

'Get up,' he grunted. 'Go, go, go.'

The dog's legs continued to move in a walking motion and they sent small stones and gravel falling down into the boy's face.

He fell backwards down the pile, taking the dog with him. It immediately sprang to its feet and continued its mad pacing.

'Stop it, Chase,' he yelled. 'What do you want me to do?' He fell to his knees. 'Please. Stop. I beg you.'

Chase hesitated and was still.

For a moment.

Then the tired animal suddenly stood up on two legs, bent its front paws downwards and began to stagger towards him.

It was begging. Walking forward on its hind legs. Still dressed in the pink parka it looked like ...

'A performing dog,' yelled the boy. 'You're doing tricks.'

The dog continued its dreadful begging walk. It was totally exhausted and began to totter.

'Stop,' said the boy. His word had no effect. He searched his mind for another. 'Freeze,' he commanded.

The poor animal stopped walking forward but remained balancing on its two back legs like a statue. It was a quivering, living sculpture.

The boy searched for other words but could find none. He recalled words that his mother had unsuccessfully used on Deefer.

'Stay.'

The dog did not move.

'Sit.'

The dog fell onto its four legs and trotted over to a low rock. It sat down on its backside like an old man taking a rest. One leg crossed over the other.

The boy hung his head, still searching for a word that would make the dog stop performing.

'Relax,' he said. 'End, over, that's enough.'

Still the dog sat in the unnatural pose with its legs crossed.

The boy dredged his mind. Finally he came up with one more word.

'Desist.'

The dog uncrossed its legs and lay panting on the ground like any pet who has returned to the fire on a cold evening after a run in the park. It glanced up him with a look that could have been gratitude.

'I wish you were mine,' said the boy.

They sat in silence for a long time. Finally the boy spoke.

'I'll tell you something, Chase. Don't beg. Some people beg because they have nothing and you can't blame them for that. But never do it just to give someone pleasure. Mum says that sort of begging is bad.'

The boy looked up and groaned as he realised his mistake.

Chase was tottering around on two legs with bent paws.

'Stop, stop, stop,' the boy yelled. 'I'm sorry. Stop. I mean desist.'

Immediately Chase fell back into a resting position. The boy scratched him behind the ear and said nothing, afraid that any word could send the poor creature into another crazy act. He searched his mind for words that he had used before that might have started the dog performing. He found five: *home, freeze, walk, sit* and *beg*.

He sat there thinking. A lightbulb popped in his head.

'The earmuffs,' he exclaimed. 'They weren't there to keep your ears warm. They were to stop you…'

He paused and looked sadly at the dog.

'I'm sorry, boy,' he said. 'I must be careful what I say.'

He reached into the backpack.

'I think you might be hungry.'

He took out the remains of the stale sandwich and dropped it in front of the dog.

The dog gulped the sandwich down and then stood up.

'I know,' said the boy. 'It's time to go. We have to find the road before dark.'

He pictured his mother preparing a meal. Trying to make the best of the cheapest food. All they could afford. He imagined her looking up at the door as she waited for him to come home.

But who was waiting for Chase? His owner was dead.

The boy stood up and put on his backpack. He was about to say, 'Home,' but thought better of it.

He pointed and the dog gave a small yelp, scrambled up the rocky pile and disappeared into the tunnel. The boy followed.

Five

In no time at all they were blinking in the daylight at the other end of the short tunnel.

The forest was fast growing dark and the boy knew that they must travel quickly.

'The race will be nearly over by now,' he said. 'And they will all be on their last lap down the mountain. We have to get back to the road.'

He looked with dismay at the remains of the railway line. The wooden sleepers had been removed long ago and the trail had vanished in the undergrowth.

'I don't know where to go,' he said to the dog. 'I'm lost. But you know the way.'

He could have saved his breath. Chase was already moving through the forest, stopping every now and then to sniff the ground.

'Yes,' yelled the boy. 'Yes, yes, yes.'

They both seemed to have found new energy but soon they were panting as they plunged down through the forest. Every now and then Chase would stop and wait for him to catch up. The boy sensed that the poor animal felt sorry for him. Or did it want something?

The last of the light glinted from the wet road as boy and dog finally broke out of the forest. Both were totally exhausted. The boy took off his backpack and sat on it. Chase dropped to the ground and curled up at his feet.

'We're safe now,' said the boy. 'Soon we can make our way ho…'

He paused and smiled and did not complete the word. But instead, '…where we want to go.'

They both stayed perfectly still, too tired to move. The dog continued to sleep so the boy sat there in silence as the evening drew closer.

'We'd better go,' the boy finally said.

But at that moment, Chase pricked up his ears and stared down the road.

'What is it?' said the boy.

A few seconds passed. And then he heard it. A siren. The sound of a vehicle coming up the mountain. An orange light blinked and flashed through the trees below. The sound grew louder.

A truck with a ladder on top rounded the bend with blaring siren and flashing lights. It slowed and then skidded to a halt.

Four men and two women in orange rescue vests were crowded into the twin cab.

The front side window dropped and a woman's friendly but serious face appeared.

'The runners have found a van up here somewhere,' she said. 'It's gone over the edge. A man and his performing dog. Do you know where they are?'

The boy opened his mouth to speak but the words wouldn't come. He opened and closed his mouth trying to force sounds from his throat. The woman looked concerned, sensing that something was wrong.

'Are you okay?' she said.

He nodded and pointed up the road.

'Thanks,' said the woman.

The driver released the brake and the van sped off and disappeared around the corner.

'You're too late,' the boy said to himself. 'The man is d…' He looked at the dog. 'Not with us anymore.'

But now the dog was looking uphill. Something else had caught its attention.

'What is it?' the boy said.

Chase gave a little whimper.

After a short while the boy heard laughing voices and the sound of feet crunching on the gravel.

It was Skinny Luke and his sister. And a group of other boys all wearing running gear and shorts.

The dog jumped nervously to its feet.

'Look who it is,' yelled Skinny Luke.

'Goldfish mouth,' said his sister.

'The Gar-bag Kid,' said Skinny Luke.

'Get a load of the dog,' said another voice. 'Wearing a parka.'

They began to laugh scornfully.

The boy looked nervously from face to face.

The gang formed a circle around the dog, which continued to whimper.

'It's the missing performing dog,' said Skinny Luke. 'Play dead,' he yelled.

The dog rolled over onto its back with its legs

sticking up stiffly, pointing to the sky. A laugh went up from the crowd.

The boy tried to push through the circle but the mob would not let him.

'Sit,' Skinny Luke shouted.

Hoots of laughter filled the air as the dog dragged itself through the crowd to a fallen log on the side of the road, sat on its backside and crossed its legs.

The boy opened his mouth to scream in protest but nothing came. The crowd laughed loudly at his agony. Two of the gang held him by the arms.

Skinny Luke's sister bent over and picked up a stick from the side of the road.

'Fetch,' she said as she hurled the stick into the forest.

The dog managed to find enough strength to trot slowly into the forest. It disappeared into the undergrowth. It was gone for some time and the forest was silent except for the sound of snuffling.

Finally it returned and wearily dropped the stick at the girl's feet.

The mob laughed and cheered.

Skinny Luke's sister picked up the stick and held it behind her head, steadying herself for the next throw.

But before she could do it another command was uttered.

'Beg.'

The exhausted dog stood up on its hind legs and began to totter with its front paws hanging down. By now the crowd was howling. Tears of mirth fell down their cheeks. Skinny Luke's sister fell to the ground holding her sides in delighted pain.

The boy ran to the dog and tried to lift it to stop the poor animal's agony. But Skinny Luke grabbed him from behind and shoved him aside.

As one command followed another the weary dog obeyed. Once again a circus act. No mind of its own. Helplessly performing one trick after another. The boy ran from one tormentor to the next. Grabbing them, pushing his hand over their mouths.

'Walk.'

'Jump.'

'Freeze.'

The dog immediately stopped begging and stood like a statue glued to the road.

The boy struggled to say something before another order could be spoken. But not a sound came from his mouth.

Skinny Luke's sister laughed scornfully.

'Spit it out,' she said.

The boy fought for words. Like a dental patient trying to answer a question with his mouth open, he could only gurgle.

'He can't do it,' said Skinny Luke.

'Can't do what?' said one of the tormentors.

Skinny Luke spat out the word gleefully.

'Speak.'

The dog immediately unfroze and began to yip. It continued with exhausted cries, yip-yapping and howling with its head turned up to the dark sky. On and on and on.

The mob fell about with laughter. They pushed and shoved each other with glee.

'It's talking,' shrieked Skinny Luke's sister.

The boy ran over to the dog and tried to hold its jaws together with his trembling fingers. Anything to stop the dreadful parody.

Suddenly the dog gave a little whimper through closed jaws and fell silent. Its eyes met the boy's, and something passed between them. There on the road in the forest, boy and dog spoke to each other without words.

Without knowing it, the boy released his hold. The dog opened its mouth again.

And found its own voice.

With lips pulled back over angry teeth the dog began to growl and crawl towards the now silent mob. The dog's angry rumble flowed towards them like molten lava. Crouching low, inching towards its persecutors with smouldering eyes it began to bark and snap. Looking at legs and soft flesh.

Darting in and out.

The terrified crowd turned and fled down the road. Falling, pushing, screaming as the dog snapped at their heels.

The mob vanished around the corner. The dog stopped and looked back at the boy and knew instinctively that the chase was over. It dropped panting by the side of the road.

The boy walked to the dog, crouched down and put his arms around the animal's neck. They were both exhausted but Chase found enough energy to raise his snout and lick the boy's face.

They sat there in silence in the deepening shadows.

Finally there was the sound of an approaching vehicle. A fire truck swept past them, slowed and stopped. It reversed back and the boy saw a blue tarpaulin on the tray of the truck. He instantly knew what lay beneath it. His legs began to tremble.

Once again a window dropped and the same woman's face appeared.

She nodded at Chase.

'Who owns that dog?' she said.

The question hung in the air unanswered.

Then the boy took a deep breath and sang his answer in a clear soprano voice. The tune was stolen but the words were his.

'It is mine. It is mine. It is mine.'

Six

It was dark when the rescue workers dropped the boy and his dog outside the front gate. He knew that he was late and his mother would be worried.

A light glowed warmly from the windows.

'We made it,' the boy said. 'You'll be safe here, Chase. But you have one last trick to work on. You have to learn *dis*obedience. I'm going to reward you for *not* doing what you're told.'

The boy paused at the tree by the gate and looked at the words scratched into its trunk. The dog seemed to sense a painful memory and rubbed against his leg.

They both stood there listening to the silence of the night until the boy noticed his mother walking swiftly down the path.

'You're late,' she said, partly cross, partly relieved. 'Why are you standing out here?'

Her gaze fell upon Chase and she sighed.

'You know we can't have another dog,' she said kindly. 'We've been through this before. It will run away and then...'

The boy began to talk in a slow rhythmic

voice, prolonging the words like a song with a beat but no tune.

'This dog is Chase,' he said. 'I will never let him go.'

She froze, unable at first to take in what was happening. Then she rushed forward and hugged him so tightly that he was unable to breathe. The tears streamed down her face.

'You're doing it,' she sobbed. 'Talking. Like they tried to show you at the clinic.'

'Relax, Mum,' he said with the same rhythmic voice.

'What's happened?' she said.

'It's a long story,' he told her. 'Let's go in. It's cold.'

They made their way inside and sat down holding hands next to the crackling fire. His mother looked at Chase, already asleep on the mat as if he had always lived there.

'You can keep the dog,' she said. 'You've had a good day...'

After a long pause she said, 'And so have I.'

'What?' he said.

She smiled.

'Even though the performing dog didn't turn up at the end of the race they still raised enough money to start up the new op shop.'

'Great,' said the boy. She smiled and he could tell there was more.

'And?' he said.

'And Skinny Luke's dad gave me the job of running it. A proper wage working in a shop.'

He rushed over and threw his arms around her.

'It's better than a thousand dollars,' he said.

After this they were happy; the boy, his mother and the dog.

Slowly and with much help the boy was able to talk more and more comfortably.

There was always wood for the fire. And a special place next to it for Chase.

Seven

A year passed and all was well, until one day there was an unexpected knock on the door.

A tall man stood there holding a pair of earmuffs. He wore the expression of a person with a task he was not looking forward to.

'I've come to talk to you about your dog,' he said.

The boy's mother invited the visitor in and offered him a seat.

He sat down and put the earmuffs on the floor.

His eyes fell upon the dog sleeping by the fire. Chase opened his eyes and sat up. At that moment the boy entered the room.

'I'm from the circus,' the man said. 'I've come for … our dog, Tricky.'

'No,' screamed the boy.

He had feared that this moment might come. But he was not ready for it. He would never be ready for it. He rushed over and squatted next to the dog. He put his arm around Chase and hugged him tightly.

The man took a deep breath and continued.

'We know Tricky's trainer died on the mountain. It's taken us a long time to track Tricky down. But finally we went to the SES and they told us they saw you with a dog just like him. The circus owns him. And we want him back.'

The boy began to tremble. But then he spoke in a firm voice.

'He is mine,' he said.

His mother looked at him sadly. She had tried to prepare him for this day.

'I'm sorry that the man died,' the boy said. 'I think about him all the time. But this dog is …'

'Ours,' the man said grimly. 'I can prove he is ours.' He reached out and picked up a small piece of wood from the fireplace and threw it across the room.

'Fetch,' he said.

The dog regarded him sleepily but didn't move.

'Walk,' he said.

Still the dog did not move.

'Play dead,' he said.

'Beg.'

Chase quivered, stood and trotted into the boy's room. He jumped onto the bed and closed his eyes, totally at peace.

There was a long silence. Clearly the man was astounded by what he saw. His lips quivered. A look of wonder came across his face.

Finally the man got to his feet, and began walking slowly towards the door. He stopped, and looked at the boy with a smile.

'I am going back to the circus empty-handed,' he said. 'But what am I going to tell them? I can't lie. Clearly it's the same dog.'

'No,' said the boy. 'Tell them he's…' He grinned and pointed to Chase, who had opened one contented eye.

'…a different dog.'

From the author

I have had a number of different occupations over the last fifty years: a special school teacher, a speech pathologist, a lecturer in reading education and an author. *A Different Dog* draws on many experiences in these fields. And of course, it also draws on my own childhood.

If you ask me, 'Where did the story come from?' that's another thing altogether. I will have to say that I don't know. It was a matter of putting my hand into the lucky dip of my own mind. There are many presents in that barrel and they are all wrapped so you don't know what you are going to get.

One of the influences on a writer would have to be the books that he or she has read themselves. An author cannot copy another's work and each writer must find their own voice. But somewhere in the back of our minds are tucked the stories we have enjoyed in the past.

Of the books that I loved when I was aged between thirteen and fifteen I can think of three which I turn back to and read again and again. They are still readily available more than fifty years later. Teenagers and adults love these stories. I still have my old copies and like to look at their torn and worn covers which beckon me from years gone by. Here they are:

Huckleberry Finn by Mark Twain. A boy and a runaway slave on the Mississippi River. How I wished I was on that raft. And little did I know that I would still be amazed by their wonderful adventures all these years later.

The Snow Goose by Paul Gallico. A girl, a bird and disabled man feature in this moving story. When you finish it you just know that there is an untold truth hinted at within the main story and it makes you think for weeks after you have read it.

The Old Man And The Sea by Ernest Hemingway. This is a lovely story about a boy, an old man and a fish. Exciting, sometimes sad but always making you ask yourself, 'Could I ever do that?'

I don't know if these authors influenced me when I wrote, *A Different Dog* but if you read any of them might like to give it some thought.

I can tell you how I think *A Different Dog* came into being. When I was eight years old, I had to bury a dead